JOURNEY TO THE CENTER OF THE EARTH 3D

The Novel

PRICE STERN SLOAN
Published by the Penguin Group
Penguin Group (USA) Inc., 375 Hudson Street, New York, New York 10014, USA
Penguin Group (Canada), 90 Eglinton Avenue East, Suite 700,
Toronto, Ontario M4P 2Y3, Canada
(a division of Pearson Penguin Canada Inc.)
Penguin Books Ltd., 80 Strand, London WC2R 0RL, England
Penguin Group Ireland, 25 St. Stephen's Green, Dublin 2, Ireland
(a division of Penguin Books Ltd.)
Penguin Group (Australia), 250 Camberwell Road, Camberwell, Victoria 3124, Australia
(a division of Pearson Australia Group Pty. Ltd.)
Penguin Books India Pvt. Ltd., 11 Community Centre,
Panchsheel Park, New Delhi—110 017, India
Penguin Group (NZ), 67 Apollo Drive, Rosedale, North Shore 0632, New Zealand
(a division of Pearson New Zealand Ltd.)
Penguin Books (South Africa) (Pty.) Ltd., 24 Sturdee Avenue,
Rosebank, Johannesburg 2196, South Africa

Penguin Books Ltd., Registered Offices: 80 Strand, London WC2R 0RL, England

Library of Congress Cataloging-in-Publication Data is available.

ISBN 978-0-8431-3230-4   10 9 8 7 6 5 4 3 2 1

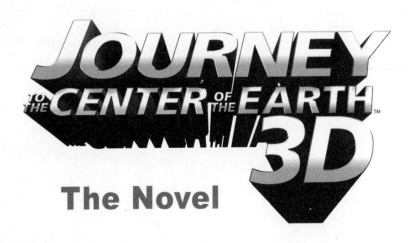

JOURNEY TO THE CENTER OF THE EARTH 3D

The Novel

Adapted by Tracey West

Based on the screenplay by Michael Weiss and
Jennifer Flackett & Mark Levin

PSS!
PRICE STERN SLOAN

The man ran through the dense jungle, his boots stomping on the tall grasses below his feet. Palm fronds scratched his face as he raced through the brush, his lungs bursting with the effort. He couldn't stop. The thing was behind him, gaining on him with each thundering step.

The thick vegetation suddenly cleared in front of him, and the man found himself skidding to a stop at the edge of a cliff. But he stumbled and lurched, falling off the cliff into a deep black chasm . . .

"Trevor! Help!"

Trevor Anderson woke up with a start, shaking from the nightmare. He took a deep breath and looked around his one-bedroom apartment, getting his bearings. Sunlight streamed through a crack in his window shades. His alarm clock read 9:17 A.M.

Trevor jumped out of bed. He was late. There was no point in dwelling—he'd had the dream about his brother Max before, but he never knew what it meant.

Trevor stumbled to the bathroom and reached for the toothpaste tube. He studied his bleary face in the mirror for a moment. He and Max had always looked alike: same brown hair, same green eyes, and same strong chin. But Max had always been neat, and the face that stared back at Trevor was, well . . . a mess. Hair that needed cutting, a face that needed shaving, teeth that needed brushing. Trevor let out a sigh.

He quickly brushed his teeth with water and ran a comb through his hair. He walked back into his bedroom, yawned, and opened the closet door. It was empty. Every item of clothing he owned was piled on the floor, waiting to be washed. He pulled on a pair of jeans and a button-down shirt that didn't smell as bad as the other shirts in the pile.

A few minutes later he headed outside, a travel coffee cup in one hand and a stack of term papers in the other. He climbed into his car and turned the key.

It wouldn't start.

So far, the day was going pretty much the same way the last hundred days had gone. No surprise there. He walked back inside and got his bicycle from the living room.

A short while later, he pedaled up to the university's campus and entered a small brick building. The sign above the door read "The Maxwell Anderson Center for the Study of Plate Tectonics."

Trevor stepped inside the lab, a small room packed with out-of-date computer equipment and monitors emitting lights and blips. His assistant, Leonard, sat at his desk eating an ice pop. When Trevor walked in, Leonard wheeled his office chair over.

"You're not going to be happy," he whispered, nodding toward Trevor's office. An uptight-looking guy in a suit sat there, waiting.

"Kitzens," Trevor muttered. Could this day get any worse? "What does he want?"

Leonard shrugged. "I don't know, but he brought his tape measure."

Trevor walked into his office. Professor Kitzens gave him a crocodile smile.

"Trevor. There's my favorite colleague," he said.

"How's that class in plate tectonics going? Does it get echoey in there with so few kids?"

"I prefer the smaller classes. It allows for a more intimate exchange of ideas," Trevor replied coolly. Kitzens knew just how to get under his skin, but he wasn't about to show he was bothered by the comment. "Now what do you want? I'm . . . you know . . . kind of busy around here."

Kitzens cast a glance at Leonard, who was leaning back in his chair, staring off into space. "Well, I'll make it quick then," he replied. "The university is pulling the plug on your brother's lab."

Trevor felt like he had been punched in the chest. "Pulling the plug?"

"We're folding it into my new Geo-Chem Institute expansion," Kitzens explained, smiling smugly. "It's going to give us the storage space we need."

Trevor stared at Kitzens, stunned. "Isn't the *dean* supposed to be giving me this information?"

Kitzen's smile got wider. "That's the other thing I'm here to tell you. I'll be Dean Kitzens, starting Thursday. It's very exciting. Now you know, if this was a 'Dean's Office Only' decision I'd let you do your little experiments forever and a day. But, you know, this is science. No one's heard anything from this lab in a very long time."

"First of all, there are no 'little experiments' going on here," Trevor countered, his voice firm. "This is a place dedicated to Max's big ideas. His seminal theories predicting volcanic fissures in the mantle—"

"—have never been proven," Kitzens pointed out. "How many of your late brother's sensors are even still working out there? One? Two?"

Trevor glanced at his computer monitor, which showed a map of the world. Max had been passionate about plate tectonics, the theory that there are large, rigid layers under the Earth's surface, constantly shifting. Before his death, Max had placed sensors in spots all over the world. The sensors recorded the movement of the plates in key spots. But Kitzens was right. Most of the sensors had stopped working years ago. Now only three dots blinked on the map: Bolivia, Mongolia, and Hawaii.

"Three," Trevor told him, as if that made any difference.

"Once upon a time it was twenty-nine," Kitzens reminded him.

Trevor threw all thoughts of dignity out the window. He couldn't just sit there and let Kitzens shut him down.

"You can't pull the plug!" he pleaded. "You do understand that without plate tectonics, everyone in the world would be living on one gigantic continent, right? You can't shut down the lab. It's all that's left of . . ."

He couldn't bear to say it.

"It's been ten years since Max died, Trevor," Kitzens said gently. "Some projects just run their course. I'm sorry, buddy."

Kitzens walked out, and Trevor helplessly watched him go. His last hope was gone.

"I'm sorry, too," he said softly.

Trevor walked out and nodded to Leonard. The lab assistant nodded back. There was nothing to say. Trevor left the lab, too depressed to keep working. What was the point?

Behind him, unseen, a fourth blip suddenly appeared on the computer screen. It pulsed faintly, but it was there . . . deep in the heart of Iceland.

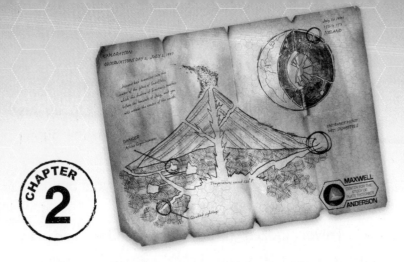

CHAPTER 2

Trevor pedaled back to his apartment. The light on his answering machine was blinking, so he pressed the button.

"Trevor, are you there? Pick up, please. Okay. Well, we're on ninety-five and heading your way." The caller's voice was agitated.

It was Elizabeth, Max's widow. Trevor got a sinking feeling. He looked over at his calendar. Written in red marker under today's date was one word: "Sean."

"Oh no," Trevor moaned. Weeks ago he'd promised that his thirteen-year-old nephew, Sean, could spend part of his summer vacation with him. But he'd forgotten all about it.

There was a beep, and another message played.

"It's your sister-in-law again. You did remember today is the day, didn't you? Sean's looking forward to seeing you, right, Sean?"

"Negatory," said his nephew in a bored tone.

Trevor frantically began to try to clean up his apartment, but it was beyond hope. Then the phone rang, and Trevor let the machine answer it.

"Trevor, we're pulling up in front of your building. Please don't let me down!"

Trevor looked through the window and saw Elizabeth's car. He stepped back, and a fleeting thought ran through his head. Maybe he could just pretend he wasn't home, and they'd go away.

He quickly dismissed the idea. Sean was his nephew, after all. There was a knock on the door.

"Trevor, are you in there?" Elizabeth called out.

Trevor took a deep breath and opened the door. His sister-in-law stood there, looking relieved and annoyed at the same time. He could see that Sean was still in the car, sulking.

"You forgot, didn't you," Elizabeth said flatly.

"What? Of course I didn't forget," Trevor responded. "You think I'd forget? Please."

Elizabeth looked past him into his filthy apartment. She wasn't convinced. "Are you sure you didn't forget?"

"Okay," Trevor blurted out. "I forgot it was *today*. But it doesn't mean I haven't been looking forward to this visit. Getting some time with my nephew, who I haven't seen since he was eleven."

"Nine," Elizabeth corrected him.

"Wow, nine, right," Trevor said. He looked at Sean again. He was a teenager now. What was he supposed to do with a teenager?

"Um, how long is he staying again?" Trevor asked.

"Ten days," Elizabeth said.

Trevor ran a hand through his hair. Ten days was a long time. But he'd promised . . .

He and Elizabeth walked up to the car. Sean didn't take his eyes off of his video game.

"Boy, am I glad to see you," Trevor said, trying to sound cheerful. "Hey, is that one of those Game Boys?"

"Sort of," Sean said, not looking up.

Elizabeth frowned. "Sean, stand up and say hi to your uncle."

Sean sighed and got out of the car. "Hi to your uncle."

Sean grabbed the duffel bag from the seat next

to him and began dragging it toward the apartment without another word. Elizabeth stopped him and gave him a hug.

"I love you," she said. "Your ticket and passport are in your bag. I'll pick you up at the airport in Ottawa. By then I'll have found a new house and we can start on our big new adventure. Pretty exciting stuff, huh?"

"We get to be Canadians," Sean said in a flat voice. "Real thrilling."

Sean headed for the front door. Elizabeth took a cardboard box out of the trunk of the car and handed it to Trevor.

"This is for you," she said. "It's Max's."

"Max's?" Trevor asked in surprise.

Elizabeth nodded. "Please take it."

Trevor took the box from her. She got into her car and drove away. Trevor followed Sean into the house and put the box on his cluttered dining table.

"Okay, man, this is going to be fun," Trevor said. "A couple of dudes hanging out, doing dude stuff."

Sean wasn't fooled by Trevor's fake positive attitude. He knew Trevor didn't want him there, and he didn't want to be there, either.

"Look, I don't like this any more than you do," Sean said. "So just keep the fridge stocked with Mountain Dew, give me the remote, and we'll get along just fine."

Trevor understood. "Let me show you around."

It didn't take long for Trevor to give Sean a tour of the small apartment. Sean didn't seem impressed by it—except for the five gigantic jars of coins in the living room.

"Wow. Nice coin collection," Sean said.

"Thanks," Trevor replied. "It's kind of a pet project."

"Nifty," Sean said flatly.

While Sean looked around, Trevor opened the box of his brother's stuff. It was filled with a bunch of old books, a yo-yo, and a framed photo of Max and Trevor together. Trevor picked up the photo.

"What's that?" Sean asked as he walked toward Trevor.

"Well, Sean, these are the possessions of a really great guy. Your dad," Trevor replied.

"Mom doesn't talk about him too much," Sean said.

Trevor pulled the yo-yo out of the box and put

the string around his finger. "This yo-yo was your father's version of a video game," he explained. He uncoiled the string, and the yo-yo swung way out in front of him. Then he reeled it back in. "Your father was a magician with this thing. He could—"

"Hey, let me try that," Sean said, and Trevor could see a spark of interest in his eyes. Sean took the yo-yo and began to play around with it while Trevor kept looking through the box. He picked up an old baseball glove and a scrapbook. Then the title of one of the books caught his eye. He picked it up.

"Wow, this was your old man's favorite book," Trevor said. "*Journey to the Center of the Earth.* Max read it to me when I was a kid."

"I think that was on my summer reading list last year. Never got to it," Sean said, flinging the yo-yo in front of him. He was shaky, but he seemed to have a natural knack for it.

Trevor opened the book. His brother had written scientific notations in the margins of the pages. "To Max, this wasn't science fiction, it was inspiration," he said. He studied the notes closely. On one page, Max had written the magma temperatures of different volcanoes around the world. 1,150 degrees in Bolivia.

718 degrees in Mongolia. 753 degrees in Hawaii.

Trevor froze. He had seen those numbers some-where before. He looked up at Sean.

"You want to see my science lab?"

The sun had set by the time they got to the lab. Trevor opened the door with his key and headed right for one of the computers. Sean trailed behind him, "walking the dog" with his yo-yo—unraveling it in front of him, then letting it roll back toward him across the floor.

"Something about the numbers in Max's book looks familiar," Trevor said, as the computer screen flashed on.

"But why can't it wait until tomorrow?" Sean asked.

"Because conditions *change*," Trevor explained. "You know what your dad used to say? He said, 'Tectonophysics isn't the science of tomorrow. It's the science of now.' It's about seismic events that occur in an instant, once a generation."

Trevor watched as numbers began to flash across the screen. "Once . . . or possibly twice," he corrected himself. He couldn't believe what he was seeing. "Look at this; it's just what I thought. Bolivia, Mongolia, Hawaii—the conditions today are almost just like they were in July ninety-seven."

"What's the big deal about July ninety-seven?" Sean asked.

Trevor held up the copy of *Journey to the Center of the Earth*, with the page opened to Max's notes.

"That was the month your dad disappeared," Trevor said. "If this was a seven hundred fifty-three instead of a seven hundred fifty-two, this whole row of numbers would . . ."

As Trevor spoke, the 752 on the screen changed to 753. Trevor turned pale.

". . . they'd be exactly the same," he said softly.

Sean was distracted by another computer. This one showed the map of the world onscreen. Lights were blinking in four different places.

"What do those little blips mean?" Sean asked. He started to press some of the buttons on the keyboard.

"Hey, don't touch that!" Trevor cried out. "Those little blips are my life's work."

"Four little blips are your life's work?" Sean asked.

"No, three little blips, actually," Trevor said.

"I count four."

Trevor rolled his office chair over to the screen. There was a fourth blip.

"Iceland," Trevor said in disbelief.

Trevor ushered a confused Sean out of the office and they went back to the apartment. Suddenly, everything made sense. He knew what he had to do. Trevor paced back and forth across the living room floor, thoughts racing in his mind.

"When Max saw the readings ten years ago, he took off to investigate," Trevor said, talking quickly as he put his jumbled thoughts together. "I never knew where. If the same conditions are repeating themselves, this could be my only chance to find out what happened."

He stopped abruptly and looked at Sean. "Where's your passport?"

"What do you need it for?" Sean asked suspiciously.

"I'm getting you to Canada a little earlier than we planned," Trevor said.

"What are you talking about?" Sean asked.

Trevor tossed the book to Sean. "*Journey to the Center of the Earth,*" he said. "It's all set in Iceland."

Sean leafed through the book. He got a little chill seeing all the notes in the margins. "This is all his writing?" he asked. Seeing it all made his father seem real, somehow.

"Max and I were talking about the possibility of long volcanic tubes stretching into the mantle. I think that's what he went looking for," Trevor said, picking up the phone. "I'm booking you a morning flight to Ottawa, and me a flight to Reykjavík."

He started to dial, but Sean pulled the cord connecting the landline to the wall. "I just got here and you already want to ditch me? I'm the one who found your life's-work-fourth-blip in the first place."

Trevor was anxious to get to Iceland. "You don't understand, Sean. He was my brother."

"He was my *father*," Sean said firmly. "I don't have to be in Ottawa for ten days."

Trevor bit his lip, thinking. Sean had a good point. And it wasn't like he was a little kid. He could handle himself in Iceland. Still . . . "Do you know how much a flight to Iceland costs at the last minute?"

Sean plugged the phone back in. He looked over his shoulder at the five giant jars of coins.

"I think you've got it covered," he said.

The next morning, Trevor and Sean were flying in a plane over the Atlantic Ocean. Sean sat in the aisle seat, practicing tricks on his yo-yo over the arm of the chair. Trevor sat next to him, carefully studying every note and mark made in Max's copy of *Journey to the Center of the Earth*. He began to read a circled passage under his breath.

"'Descend bold traveler into the crater of the Jokul of Snaeffels, which the shadow of Scartaris touches before the kalends of July, and you will attain the center of the Earth.'"

Sean sighed, finally bored with the yo-yo. He looked over at his uncle, who was now scribbling on a pile of napkins.

"What are you doing?" Sean asked.

"Your old man drew all these notations that I can't decipher," Trevor answered. "I am trying to decode this series of paired letters. Some of them are elements. Like RN, for example, I know is radon."

Sean looked down at the page his uncle was working on. Two long strands of letters were written in the margin.

"Sigurbjörn?" Sean said out loud. The first line looked like some kind of word or name.

"What did you say?" Trevor asked.

Sean pointed to the letters. "Sigurbjörn Ásgeirsson? It's right there. Just read down."

"Oh, um, right," Trevor said. "Wow. Thanks. But what does it mean? Is it a place? Or a name? Actually, it looks kind of familiar."

Trevor flipped through the book. His brother had written an address on the back of the last page. The address was for a place called the Ásgeirsson Institute for Progressive Volcanology.

"Max must have been in touch with him," Trevor said, his voice rising with excitement. "Maybe this guy saw Max before he disappeared. I knew there was a reason I brought you, kid!"

CHAPTER 4

The desolate landscape of Iceland stretched out in all directions as they drove down the highway. They had already driven through miles and miles of treeless tundra, and from the looks of things, they had many more miles to go. Sean struggled to make sense of the map they'd bought at the airport.

"You sure we're going the right way?" Trevor asked nervously.

"How should I know?" Sean asked. "I can't read Icelandic. But I think there's just this one main highway. It should take us to that volcano place."

Sean gazed out the window. The land was barren, but it was beautiful at the same time. The grass on the plains was a deep shade of green. The sky was streaked in deep oranges and reds as the sun set. Even though it was beautiful, Sean couldn't help being bored as mile after mile flew by.

"Are we there yet?" he asked.

"No, we're not there yet," Trevor replied.

Sean paused. "Now?" he joked.

"No!" Trevor snapped. "Not now!" The long hours of travel were starting to get to him, too.

"You're driving kind of slow, man," Sean pointed out.

Trevor frowned. "I'm driving kind of *safe*."

"I just saw a goat in the passing lane," Sean said without missing a beat.

Trevor scowled. They drove in silence for a while. Sean shifted in his seat.

"When's the 'adventure' part going to begin?" he asked.

"Hey, we've been together a day and we're already in Iceland! What does it take to entertain you kids these days?" Trevor wondered. He squinted at the windshield. A white fog was rising from the ground. "The 'adventure' part begins just as soon as we find Sigurbjörn Ásgeirsson."

They drove on. The sun set, and the fog became as thick as soup. Trevor plodded on slowly, searching for some indication of civilization.

"You'd think the Ásgeirsson Institute for Progressive Volcanology might have a couple signs leading to it," he muttered.

"How do you know we're not there right now?" Sean pointed out. "We could be in the parking lot for all we know."

Then Trevor slammed on the brakes, and the car bumped into a wooden sign that had a familiar name on it: ÁSGEIRSSON. Just past the sign they could make out a small one-room shack on the side of the road.

Trevor grinned. This must be the institute. And to a scientist, every lab or workstation was appreciated—even if it was incredibly small.

"Alrighty," Trevor said. "Not too shabby, eh?"

They parked the car and made their way through the fog to the shack. Although it was the last day of June, it was chilly. The warmer summer temperatures of Iceland hadn't quite kicked in yet.

The wood steps creaked as they walked up to the front door. Trevor knocked.

"Sigurbjörn Ásgeirsson? Hello?" he called out.

A muffled female voice responded from inside.

The woman was speaking Icelandic.

"I'm a scientist from America," Trevor said, speaking even louder. "I'm looking for Sigurbjörn Ásgeirsson."

The woman shouted another foreign reply. Trevor shook his head. "I'm sorry. I don't speak Ice—"

The door opened, and a beautiful young woman stood there. She had blond hair that shone like gold in the light of the cabin, and her blue eyes stared at them curiously.

"Can I help you?" she asked.

Trevor was startled. "You . . . you speak English."

"Yes, as well as French, Finnish, Croatian, and in a pinch, a little Farsi," she said matter-of-factly. She held out her hand. "I'm Hannah."

Trevor shook her hand, staring at her like a man under a spell. "I'm Trevor Anderson, Professor of Tectonics, visiting from America with my nephew, uh . . ."

"Sean," Sean reminded him.

"Right. Sean," Trevor said. "We're looking for Sigurbjörn Ásgeirsson."

"Sigurbjörn Ásgeirsson is dead," Hannah replied.

Her expression was as cold and calm as newly fallen snow. "Three winters ago."

"I see," Trevor said, his hopes fading. "Did you work for him?"

"He was my father," Hannah said, and there was a trace of sadness in her voice.

"Oh. I'm sorry," Trevor said. "So, who runs the Institute now?"

Hannah's face clouded. "There is no Institute. Progressive volcanology was a failed idea, like the Berlin Wall or eight-track tapes." She eyed them suspiciously. "What business did you have with my father?"

Trevor wasn't sure how to respond. His brother's disappearance was a long story—and a strange one at that. Thankfully, Sean broke the awkward silence.

"It sure smells good in there," he said, gazing into the cozy-looking cabin.

Hannah softened at the sight of Sean shivering in the cold. "I was just stirring a pot of hot chocolate. Would you like some?"

"Yes, please," Sean answered gratefully.

He and Trevor nearly collided in their hurry

to follow Hannah inside. Soon they were seated at Hannah's small kitchen table. Trevor slid Max's copy of *Journey to the Center of the Earth* across the table to her.

"Yeah, I know it," she said. The blank look returned to her face. "So what about it?"

"This was my late brother's book," Trevor replied. "His name was Max Anderson. And we believe he was in contact with your father."

"Your brother was a Vernian?" Hannah asked.

Sean was curious. "What's a Vernian?"

"A Vernian is what I call members of La Société de Jules Verne, a group of fanatics who believed the writing of Jules Verne was actual fact. I mean, the guy was a science *fiction* writer. But these believers regarded him as visionary. My father was the biggest Vernian of all," she explained. "A Vernian is a fool."

"Well, my brother was no fool," Trevor insisted.

Hannah picked up Max's copy of the book and glanced at all of the notations he'd made.

"Oh yes," she said. "Your brother was definitely a believer. Big-time. Check this out."

She walked to a bookshelf and took down a hardcover copy of *Journey to the Center of the Earth* that looked quite old. She handed it to Trevor. He opened it, and saw that it was a first edition—very rare.

"This was my father's," she said.

Trevor flipped through the book. The notes in the margins were almost identical to Max's notes.

Sean was a little freaked out. "Wow," he said. "My father was . . . out there."

"You didn't know him, Sean," Trevor said defensively.

"Apparently, neither did you," Sean shot back.

"I knew he liked the book, but I didn't know he was part of a secret society," Trevor said.

Hannah studied both of them as they argued. "Why are you two way out here?" she asked. "You two are not Vernians, are you?"

Trevor and Sean looked at each other. They were trying to find out what happened to Max—and he was a Vernian—but Hannah didn't need to know exactly why they were here. Trevor had a feeling she wouldn't appreciate the truth.

"Us? Vernians? Of course not," Trevor replied.

"Because I do not suffer fools gladly," Hannah warned.

Trevor scrambled for an explanation. "I . . . I'm a professor and a scientist. There's a seismic sensor going off thirty clicks north of here that I think is, um . . . worth checking on. That's why we've come out here."

"There are no roads out to the north," Hannah said.

Trevor nodded. "I kind of had a feeling about that."

"Well, I am a guide. A mountain guide. I will take you there, Professor," Hannah offered.

"Excellent," Trevor said, smiling with relief. He and Sean might find some answers after all. "And please, call me Trevor."

"And call me Sean," Sean added.

"So how much do you charge?" Trevor asked.

"To go there?" Hannah said. "Five thousand kronor."

Trevor winced. "A day?"

"An hour," Hannah replied.

"Steep rate," Trevor sighed, but he knew he had no choice.

Hannah smiled slyly. "Helps to be the only one out here."

Sean grinned. "Do you accept rolls of quarters?"

CHAPTER 5

The next morning they set out across the tundra. In the daylight, Sean and Trevor could make out tall mountaintops rising from the horizon. The snow-covered peaks looked majestic—and high. They'd only been hiking for a few hours, but Trevor and Sean were already winded from the high altitude and low temperature. Hannah, on the other hand, looked like she was on a leisurely stroll in the park. She was yards in front of them.

"If you could, just slow down there by a degree, Hannah," Trevor called out.

"I . . . I don't think she can hear you," Sean said, gasping for breath. "She's too far ahead of us." He bent over and grabbed his knees, sucking in the cold air.

Trevor stopped. "Come on, don't let her see you

rest," he said, but he was panting, too. "I thought you were this tough kid."

"In Orange, New Jersey, I'm a tough kid," Sean wheezed. "In Iceland I . . . need oxygen."

Hannah's voice echoed back to them. "Move! I want to be home by sundown!"

They both looked up, unbelieving, at the sight of Hannah so far in the distance.

They all hiked on for another hour. A wickedly cold wind kicked up, howling across the tundra. Dark clouds were beginning to roll across the sky. The only welcome sight was Hannah, who had finally stopped.

"Is your seismic sensor within range?" she asked.

Trevor looked at the small global positioning system device in his hand. "Looks like we're getting close," he said, trying to conceal his shortness of breath from Hannah.

She surveyed the landscape around them, and Trevor detected a slight wistfulness in her eyes.

"Before the mines caved in, this mountain was once very busy," she said.

They arrived near the spot where the sensor was hidden. Trevor's exhaustion from the hike was suddenly replaced with new energy. The answers to a ten-year-old mystery lay somewhere on this mountain.

"Yeah, so which peak is Snaeffels?" he asked, trying to sound casual.

"This peak," Hannah replied. "We are atop Snaeffels."

"What's Snaeffels?" Sean asked.

Hannah's blue eyes pierced Trevor. "Tell him, Professor. Please."

Trevor chose his words carefully. "Snaeffels is a mountain—well, an old volcano, really," he said. "And in Verne's ridiculous science *fiction* book, this character Lidenbrock supposedly finds this portal to the center of the Earth there."

From the expression on Hannah's face, Trevor knew that she suspected he was a Vernian in disguise. And he wasn't. Well, not really. But a thought had been forming in the back of his mind. What if Max had really found the portal? That would explain his disappearance.

"Let's just find that sensor of yours, Professor," Hannah said. "The weather is turning."

Trevor scanned the area for some sign—any sign at all. "Give me a minute," he said.

"We must get going," Hannah said sharply. She shivered. "I do not like it up here. Especially on the kalends."

"Did you say 'the kalends'?" Trevor asked.

Hannah began to hike away from them. "Yes. Today is July first, the kalends of July. But you wouldn't know that, would you, Trevor? Because you're not a Vernian, right?"

Sean followed after Hannah, but Trevor hung back. He had the passage from Verne memorized by now.

". . . in the center of the Jokul of the Snaeffels when the shadow of Scartaris touches, at the kalends of July, you will attain the center of the Earth," he whispered.

Then he heard Sean shout from up ahead. "Trevor! Your sensor! I think I see it!"

Trevor hurried up ahead. Sean was right. A thick metal cylinder emerged from the rocks, the red light on top blinking rhythmically. He took a key from his pocket and began to pry at the object's seams.

"What are you doing with it?" Hannah asked.

"Trying to disengage the cylinder," Trevor explained. "The entire seismic history of the last decade is embedded inside here. If I download the black box, the readings might tell me what kind of activity transpired when Max was here."

A cold wind swept across the mountain ridge. Sean looked up at the sky, which was growing darker with storm clouds. Hannah noticed them, too.

"How long is this going to take?" she asked. "The weather's turning. We have to go back."

"Hard to tell," Trevor said, still working at the metal. "There's a lot of corrosion."

Without warning, a powerful boom of thunder shook the very Earth they stood on.

"Trevor! We need to take cover!" Hannah shouted. "Come on, Sean."

She grabbed Sean's hand and headed to a nearby cave. But Trevor ignored her. He was so close to getting the data he needed. He wasn't going to give up now.

Boom! The sky exploded with another clap of thunder. Sheets of rain poured down from the sky.

"I almost got it!" Trevor cried, refusing to give up. "Just another minute!"

Hannah and Sean watched Trevor from the mouth of the cave. Hannah shook her head.

"He's as crazy as my father was," she whispered to herself.

Rain pounded Trevor, soaking through his clothes, as he gave the cylinder one last pull. It came off in his hand. He held it up victoriously.

"Got it!" he yelled.

Crack! A jagged streak of lightning careened across the sky, landing in the dirt just a few feet from Trevor. He finally realized the danger he was in.

"Uncle Trevor!" Sean screamed.

"Get in here!" Hannah yelled.

"I'm fine!" Trevor shouted back, but another ear-splitting crack of thunder drowned him out. The lightning struck even closer to him this time.

"Trevor! Drop the sensor!" Hannah cried out in alarm. The metal cylinder was a perfect lightning rod. Just one zap, and Trevor would be electrocuted.

But Trevor couldn't hear her over the rain and wind. "What?"

He ran for the cave, clutching the sensor in his arms.

"Drop it!" Hannah screamed, but Trevor still couldn't hear. He stuffed the sensor into his bag.

Another rumble of thunder shook the

mountaintop. Trevor dove for the mouth of the cave. His bag rolled on the ground next to him.

Crack! A lightning bolt found the sensor in Trevor's backpack. The whole cave shook as the electricity made impact with the cylinder. Rocks and dirt tumbled from the walls and ceiling, and the cave entrance collapsed.

The explosion knocked Trevor to the floor of the cave. He lay there for a moment, stunned. The inside of the cave was pitch black. He sat up, groggy.

"Sean?" he asked.

"I . . . I'm okay." Sean's voice was a little shaky.

Trevor rose to his feet. "Hannah?" he called out.

A white flashlight beam pierced the darkness. "Everybody, let's just stay calm—" she began.

But Sean was far from calm. He gripped the enormous boulders that blocked the entrance, trying to push them out of the way.

"Guys! Help! Please! Let's dig!" he urged.

Trevor joined him, and even Hannah pitched in, chipping at the rock with her walking stick.

"Forget it," she said quickly. "It's no use."

"What do you mean, forget it?" Sean asked, panic in his voice.

Trevor let go of the boulder. "She's right. There must be sixty tons of rock here. It would take us months to dig our way out. We'll have to find another way."

"What if there's not another way?" Sean asked.

Hannah looked around the cave. From her bag, she took out three headlamps—each had a light attached to a strap to be worn around the head.

"There's always another way, Sean," she assured him.

Trevor raised an eyebrow, impressed. "What else you got in that bag?"

"Signal flares. First aid. Rope. A blanket," Hannah said. "A couple of protein bars, but they are on ration. We have no idea how long we will be trapped."

"Trapped?!" Sean's eyes were wild. "Is that what we are?"

He flipped open his cell phone and frantically started to dial. Trevor put an arm on his shoulder.

"Sean," he said softly.

"What? I'm not getting any signal!" Sean cried.

"We're on the top of a mountain, buried under magnetically charged rock," Trevor told him. "Of course there's no signal."

Sean looked really scared. Trevor knew he had to try to make him feel more confident.

"Sean, we're going to get out, all right?" he promised. "I promised your mom I'd take care of you, and I'm going to keep that promise."

"Somehow, not entirely comforting," Sean muttered.

Hannah pointed her flashlight into the darkness of the cave. "Come on," she said. "Let's find the other way."

They all strapped on their headlamps, and Trevor and Sean followed Hannah down the tunnel at the back of the cave. They walked for several yards and then came to a fork in the tunnel. It was impossible to see what waited ahead for them in either narrow passageway.

"One of them might snake up to the surface," Hannah suggested.

"Which one do we take?" Sean asked.

"My gut says go right," Trevor said confidently.

Hannah frowned, unsure, so Trevor took the

lead. Trevor bragged as they walked down the tunnel. "Yeah, this looks like the way. I always had a nose for this stuff. Direction is like my sixth sense."

The tunnel took a turn, and they all had to duck around some jagged rocks protruding out of the wall. The turn took them right into a dead end.

"Turn around. Back the way we came," Trevor said, trying to sound like he knew what he was talking about.

"So what's your seventh sense?" Sean teased.

Hannah turned around. "From now on, you follow me."

Sean looked up at Trevor. "My mom's going to go prehistoric on you when she hears about this little road trip of ours."

"I hope I'm there to see that," Hannah quipped.

"For the record," Trevor shot back, "I'm not the one who led us into this cave."

"No, but you are the one who led us up to this mountain on the kalends," Hannah said.

The mood was tense as they made their way back through the tunnel. When they came back to the fork in the path, they entered the other tunnel. It was their only option.

Hannah led the way as they squeezed past stalactites and stalagmites protruding from the floor and ceiling.

"You know, I've missed this—the field work," Trevor said, as they hiked the twisting and turning path. "I've been cooped up in the lab all these years."

"Yeah, being caught inside a volcano is so much better," Sean said.

Trevor became distracted by a pattern he noticed in the rock wall. "Crystalline striations," he said, with wonder in his voice. "I wouldn't have expected to see anything like this down here."

He stepped ahead, entranced by the wall, when he suddenly felt Hannah yank him back by his shoulder.

"Watch out!" she cried.

Trevor looked down, startled. The path ended a few steps in front of him—and dropped into a deep, black chasm. He would have plummeted to his death.

Trevor caught his breath. "Thanks."

Hannah nodded. "You owe me one."

They all looked over the edge of the cliff. Even with their headlamps, they couldn't see the bottom of the drop.

"Do you think this leads down to the center of

the Earth?" Sean joked.

Hannah smirked. Trevor saw an old wooden plank on the ground and picked it up. Icelandic letters had been carved into the wood. "What's this say?" he asked Hannah.

"*Vicurvaeri ut,*" she answered. "Keep out."

"Maybe that's, um, decent advice," Sean guessed.

"No, it's good news," Hannah said. "It might lead us into an old mine shaft, and be our way out of here."

"How deep do you think that is?" Sean asked nervously.

Trevor had an idea. He asked Hannah for one of the flares. He banged the tip across the surface of the ground and it sparked to life.

"Sean, I'm going to drop the flare," he said. "Look at your watch and tell me how many seconds pass before it stops."

Trevor moved to drop the flare, when the fiery red sparks touched the wall behind them. The wall burst into flame! Hannah, Trevor, and Sean hit the dirt.

Trevor stared at the flare in his hand, then the wall where the miniature explosion had been.

"Magnesium," he realized. "There must be veins running all over these walls."

"And magnesium is kind of . . . flammable, Professor?" Hannah asked.

"It's, um, used in gunpowder," Trevor said.

Hannah took the flare away from Trevor and put it out. She stood up and retrieved a glow stick from her bag.

"Same principle," Trevor said, his pride hurt.

"With slightly less chance of blowing our heads off," Hannah pointed out. She handed it to Trevor. He dropped it down the chasm, and Sean kept time on his watch. After a moment, they heard the stick hit bottom.

"Three seconds," Sean reported. "That's good, right?"

"Thirty-two feet per second squared, that's two hundred feet," Trevor said. "Your basic twenty-story high-rise."

"Two hundred. No problem," Hannah said, taking out a long rope.

"Whoa—no problem for what?" Sean asked. He had a feeling he knew the answer.

"Rappelling down in there," Hannah said calmly.

Sean panicked. "Rappelling? You mean climbing down in that deep dark hole?"

"Your father was a gifted climber," Trevor assured him. "It's in your DNA."

"Well, guess what? I didn't get that gene," Sean said. "There's no way we should be rappelling down there into darkness!"

"Come on, Sean," pleaded Trevor. "You can do this."

Sean knew he had no choice. His palms began to sweat as Hannah attached the ropes to a protruding rock at the top of the cliff. Then she secured a rappelling harness to each of them. They were all tethered to the same rope.

"I'll go first," Trevor offered. He took a deep breath, then began to climb down the chasm. Hannah followed him. Sean hesitated for a moment, not sure if he could do it. But it was either climb down, or be stuck in the cave forever.

He started to climb. His sweaty hands gripped the rope tightly as he used his feet to feel for cracks and grooves in the rock wall. He tried not to look down.

Several minutes later, he heard his uncle's voice

from below. "Look at all this schist!"

"What?" Sean called down.

"Schist," Trevor called back. "It's a metamorphic rock. Oh noooooo—"

A stone broke under Trevor's foot. He free-fell backward, straight down into the darkness. His rope line jerked tightly, tangling with Hannah's line. She strained under the weight.

Hannah kicked her feet into the wall to secure her position. She had to think quickly. Trevor would pull them all down if they didn't do something.

"Trevor, get to a wall!" she shouted.

Trevor looked around him. The nearest wall was a few yards away. "I can't!" he shouted back.

"Your rope is attached to us," Hannah said. "You're going to take us all down. I'm going to have to cut you loose!"

"What?" Trevor wailed.

Hannah pulled a knife from her pack. She swiftly and expertly cut the rope. Trevor screamed in terror as he plummeted to the bottom of the chasm.

Sean and Trevor begin their journey on a plane to Iceland.

Trapped inside the volcano.

A wild waterslide deposits them deep underground.

Welcome to the center of the Earth!

Sean's dad was right all along!

Inside the Mushroom Forest.

A raft ride down the river may be their only way to escape.

This little glowbird helps Sean find his way back to the river.

Sean surfs the sky on giant magnetic stones.

Run, Trevor, run!

Dinosaur skull boat—the only way to travel!

This is one journey they'll never forget!

"Aaaaaaaaaaaaah!"

Trevor fell—about two feet. He landed with a dull thud.

"The, uh, bottom's right here, guys," he said sheepishly.

Hannah dropped down behind him. She unhooked her harness and lowered Sean down beside them.

"You knew that, right, Hannah?" Trevor asked.

Hannah didn't answer—but Trevor thought he saw a slight smile in her blue eyes. He hoped he did, anyway.

They had landed in front of another tunnel entrance.

"Where are we?" Sean asked.

"Abandoned mine tunnel," Trevor replied.

"Old Bla'gils Mine," Hannah said. "They shut it

down sixty years ago. After the big disaster."

"Uh, how big?" Sean asked.

"Eighty-one dead," Hannah said.

"That's pretty big," Trevor remarked.

But it was their only hope of a way out. They all walked down the dusty tunnel, dirt crunching underneath their feet. Sean lagged behind Trevor and Hannah.

"Where did you learn to speak English so well?" Trevor asked her.

"I went to boarding school in London," Hannah explained. "The best thing my father ever did for me was to send me away."

"Now that he's gone, are you happy to be back home?" Trevor asked.

"I'm an Icelander," she replied. "If we Icelanders do not return, there will be no more Iceland."

Hannah seemed comfortable talking to him, finally. Trevor took advantage of the moment.

"Hannah, do you ever wonder if . . . you know . . . just in theory . . . what if my brother and your father weren't wrong?"

Hannah stopped cold. She turned to Trevor. "Let me make something clear," she said, her voice like ice.

"I'm not my father."

"I never said—"

"The world he belonged to has nothing to do with me," Hannah insisted. "He died in an asylum in Oslo still raving about the center of the Earth. That, my friend, will never happen to me."

"I understand," Trevor said, trying to repair the damage. "I only meant—"

"I'm still on the clock, you know," Hannah informed him.

"Wait, you're billing me for this?" Trevor asked.

"I'm billing you until I'm back, safe in my house," Hannah said. Then she turned and walked ahead of him.

Sean caught up to Trevor. "What were you two talking about?" he asked. Suddenly Hannah's voice rang through the passage.

"Over here!"

They ran ahead and found Hannah standing next to a bank of levers attached to a huge metal machine. It looked like it had been built a hundred years ago.

"What is it?" Sean asked.

Hannah reached for a lever. "The old generator

for the mine."

"Sure you want to pull that, Hannah?" Trevor asked nervously.

Hannah ignored him and yanked on the lever, then flipped a switch. The old generator wheezed to life. Floodlights began to sputter on, illuminating the underground cavern with pale yellow light. They could see a few old mine cars lined up on the track. Sean felt relief for the first time since the cave entrance had collapsed.

"This is what we're looking for, right?" he asked. "The miners, they had to get their stuff out somewhere, right? So these tracks should take us out."

Trevor couldn't help thinking of the "big disaster" Hannah had described. "Hannah, did any of the miners get out?" he asked.

"Yes. One," she answered simply.

Sean hopped into the lead mine car. "Well, that's a start. I call front."

"Sean, out," Trevor ordered. "We're walking the track."

"But we've been walking forever," Sean pointed out.

"But we don't even know if these things work,"

Trevor said.

Hannah drove up in a pump car, proving him wrong. She banged into the mining car in front of her. "The track looks good," she said. "Get in."

The cart wheels squeaked on the track as they began to rumble slowly through the mine shaft. Sean sat in the first car, clearly enjoying the adventure. Trevor followed behind him, looking nervous. Hannah brought up the rear in the pump car.

Sean stood up and craned his neck to get a better view.

"Watch it, kid," Trevor warned. "That's not safe there."

"But I think I see something," Sean said. "It's—"

He quickly sat down. Up ahead, the track took a deep dip into a massive cavern.

"Uh-oh," Sean said.

The cars lurched forward, dropping down into a tremendous mining cavern. The train tracks branched in every direction, running on steel supports suspended in midair. It was like they were on some kind of sinister roller coaster.

"Everybody keep your arms and legs inside the

car at all times!" Trevor called out.

Sheer momentum sent the carts hurtling down the track. They snaked and looped through the track at a dizzying speed. Sean cried out in terror and joy. Hannah smiled for the first time since Trevor and Sean had appeared on her doorstep. Only Trevor looked miserable.

The carts whipped around a sudden, sharp curve. Up ahead, Sean could clearly see a gap in the tracks! Crushed and broken mining cars were scattered on the floor of the cavern below.

"Hannah!" he screamed.

"I know!" she called out.

"Pull the brakes!" Trevor yelled, but Hannah disagreed.

"Don't! We won't make it!"

Hannah pumped her cart as fast as she could. She knew only sheer speed would get the carts across the gap.

Sean's cart hit the gap first. He held his breath as the carts flew . . . and flew . . . until . . .

WHAM! The carts slammed into the track on the other side. Nobody was hurt. Trevor couldn't believe it.

"That was incredible," Trevor said, looking back at Hannah as the carts rumbled along. "Thank—"

There was a loud click and Sean's cart unhooked from Trevor's. The cars had reached a three-way fork, and Sean went down the track on the right.

Trevor's cart split off next, careening down the track on the left. Hannah's pump cart kept going right down the middle.

The three carts raced side by side down the tracks. Trevor's cart rattled as the track below him became bumpy and rough. He pulled a handle, thinking it was the brake, but instead the door on the back of the cart fell open. Trevor quickly pulled the door closed and tried another handle. This time, his cart began to spin wildly, like a crazy tilt-a-whirl.

"Whoooaaaaa!" Trevor cried.

Trevor's stomach lurched as he struggled to get the cart back under control. He finally stopped the spinning.

"Are you okay?" Hannah called over to him.

Trevor gave the thumbs-up—and then noticed the edge of a sheer cliff up ahead, where Hannah's track abruptly ended.

"Hannah! Your track! Quick! Jump in!"

Hannah hesitated. Then she bravely jumped into Trevor's car. He caught her in his arms.

"You're something else," he said, smiling.

Hannah smiled back—then her face went as white as a sheet as she caught sight of something up ahead.

"Trevor, this track ends, too!"

Trevor looked and saw a wall of solid rock a few yards in front of them. Hannah grabbed a rope in the mine car and threw the attached anchor out of the car.

"What are you doing?" Trevor asked.

Hannah tied the rope around herself and Trevor. "Showing you the proper way to save someone's life."

"How is that going to—*Aaaaaaaaah!*"

The anchor got caught in the rocks below, jerking Hannah and Trevor out of their cart. They slammed into the track, but the cart had a much worse fate. It plowed through the face of the rock wall, exploding into splinters. Bits of rock rained down on Hannah and Trevor on the track.

"Are you okay?" Trevor asked. He stood up, brushing dust off of his pants.

"I'm fine," Hannah said, jumping to her feet.

"That's two you owe me."

"Who's keeping track?" Trevor asked.

"I am," Hannah replied.

Sean rolled up in his cart on the track behind them, using his hand brake to come to an easy stop.

"That. Was. Awesome!" he cried, jumping up. "What happened to you guys?"

Hannah and Trevor didn't answer. They were staring at the hole in the rock wall. As the dust cleared, they could see it led into a large cave.

"What is that?" Sean wondered, walking to the wall.

"Sean, come back from there!" Trevor cried.

"What are you talking about?" Sean asked. "It could be a way out."

Then he disappeared through the opening.

Sean adjusted his headlamp to get a better view of the cave. The light shone on a wall of gleaming red crystals. He couldn't believe it.

"Guys, check it out!" he cried out. "Rubies!"

Trevor and Hannah entered the cave. Hannah flashed her lamp on another wall. This one illuminated shining green jewels.

"Emeralds!" she cried.

Trevor's light shone on a wall that looked plain, but he recognized the stone right away. "Feldspar!" he exclaimed excitedly.

Sean gave Trevor a funny look, but he was soon distracted when he discovered another chamber in the cave. Clear, shining jewels shone from every surface—in the wall, in the ceiling, piled on the ground.

"Diamonds," Hannah whispered.

The precious gems glittered all around them. Trevor looked around, awestruck.

"Must be volcanic tubes," he said. "High temperatures in volcanic tubes enable the formation of crystals."

Sean picked up two diamonds off the floor. He held them up next to Hannah.

"Hey, these would make a nice pair of earrings for you," he said.

"Thank you, Sean," she said. Then she sighed a little. "But all this is worth nothing if we can't find our way out of here."

Sean was busy shoving diamonds into his pockets. "Still, if we get out, I'm getting a Maserati."

Trevor scanned the cavern, wondering how this treasure trove was formed.

"These diamonds must have been pushed up by magma, and that's how they rose to the surface," he guessed. "We must be close to the center of the crater."

"Could the crater be our escape?" Hannah wondered.

"What we'd be looking for is some kind of vent

up above," he said, gazing up at the ceiling. He took a step forward.

Craaaack! The loud sound startled them all. They looked down at their feet to see thin, spiderweb cracks forming beneath them.

"Um, anybody else feel that?" Sean asked.

"Stop moving," Trevor said urgently.

"What is it?" Hannah asked, frozen in position.

"Muscovite," Trevor answered. As he spoke, the thin fractures in the floor began to intersect with one another.

"What's muscovite?" Sean asked.

Hannah's face was troubled. She knew the answer. "It's a very thin type of rock formation."

"*How* thin?" Sean asked nervously. The thrill of finding the diamonds had quickly disappeared.

"So thin that the slightest change in weight or pressure can shatter it," his uncle answered. "In fact, it got its name from the Russians, who used it for, um . . . glass."

"I'm sure your students find that kind of fascinating," Sean said, his voice shaking a little. "But I'm more worried about standing on glass."

The sound of the cracking faded.

"It stopped," Hannah whispered.

"Okay," Trevor said. "Now, very carefully people."

Very slowly, Trevor, Hannah, and Sean made their way back to the entrance of the cavern. They took one careful step after another. Soon they were just a few feet away . . .

Clink!

A diamond fell from Sean's backpack. Everyone held their breath as it landed on the fragile floor. A second passed. Nothing happened.

"Must be thicker than I thought," Trevor said gratefully.

He spoke too soon.

An ear-splitting *CRAAAACK* echoed through the cavern. The muscovite shattered, and the floor fell out from under their feet.

"*Aaaaaaaahh!*" Sean screamed.

"*Aaaaaaaahh!*" Hannah yelled.

"*Aaaaaaaahh!*" Trevor wailed.

They were falling, falling into the darkness.

They kept falling . . .

Then they fell some more . . .

They all wondered the same thing at the same

time: Why hadn't they hit bottom?

A strange calm came over the group. Sean reached out and grabbed hands with Trevor and Hannah. They were floating through the empty space, almost like skydivers sailing on the wind. But unlike the skydivers, they didn't have parachutes.

"Will someone tell me why we're not, like, splatting at the bottom?" Sean yelled.

"Our minds are stretching out the final, fleeting moments of our lives," Hannah guessed. "This is all happening in the blink of an eye."

Trevor had a different idea. "Or we're just falling really, really far . . ."

A strange curiosity came over them as they continued to plummet down what appeared to be a bottomless pit.

"What's at the bottom?" Sean asked.

"Well, if Jules Verne was right, some of these tunnels go hundreds, maybe thousands of miles," Trevor said.

"But Verne was *not* right," Hannah said firmly.

"Trevor! Finish!" Sean pleaded, looking down at the endless-looking pit. "What's at the bottom?"

"I don't know," Trevor admitted. "The most

likely theory is it probably just . . . ends."

Panic gripped Sean once again. "*Ends?* Got any other theories?"

"Well, the, um, sides of this tunnel could gently slope, eroded by water, which could still run through it," Trevor said, digging for any theory that might give them hope. "The water could provide a gradual breaking of our fall, sort of like . . . a waterslide."

This definitely cheered up Sean a bit. "Waterslide? Okay. Now that's a theory!"

Hannah didn't get that Trevor was trying to make Sean feel better. "But Trevor, what if the water formed stalagmites that are pointing straight up at us?" she asked. "We'd be skewered at one hundred eighty miles per hour."

"*Aaaaaahh!*" Sean screamed again.

The three travelers continued to plunge down the tunnel. Something splashed on Sean's face from below. He looked down.

"What is that?" he wondered out loud.

Big globules of water were floating *up* the tunnel. That meant there was water below. Trevor's theory might be right!

"Waterslide, waterslide, waterslide," Sean whispered.

The thunderous sound of rushing water greeted them. Trevor didn't know if it was a waterslide—but they were definitely about to get wet.

"Everyone grab hold!" he yelled.

Trevor, Hannah, and Sean plunged into a funnel of water that wrapped around them and sent them swirling to the bottom of the water. They struggled to hold hands, but the splashing water was too powerful for them. First Sean lost his grip, then Hannah.

Trevor couldn't scream, couldn't swim, and couldn't fight in the roaring current. The water would either carry them all to safety—or this would be the end of their journey.

The water submerged Trevor on all sides, but it was suddenly calm. He saw a dim light up ahead—the water's surface? He swam with all his might.

He emerged from the water, gasping for breath. He appeared to be in some kind of lagoon in a dark underground cave.

Sean popped out of the water next, taking big gulps of air.

"Whoa, we didn't get skewered," he said, amazed.

But Trevor wasn't ready to celebrate yet. "Where's Hannah?"

They looked around the lagoon, but there was no sign of her.

"Get to shore, Sean!" Trevor urged. He dove under the water just as Hannah popped back up. She gasped for air and then went back under.

"I can't find her," Trevor said, coming to the surface.

"She's right next to you!" Sean said.

Hannah suddenly popped up again. "My pack. Too heavy."

Trevor wrestled the straps from around her shoulders. They swam to the rocky shore and then collapsed, exhausted.

"How many do I owe you now?" Trevor asked.

"You're back to one," Hannah said, smiling.

"Ottawa's sounding pretty good about now," Sean added.

They lay there in silence for a moment, feeling lucky to be alive—and confused about where they were.

As they stared at the dark ceiling of the cave, they noticed that mysterious blue lights were gently flickering above them. Hundreds of lights sparkled like tiny stars.

"Those look like . . . stars?" Hannah asked, hopeful for a moment. But she knew it couldn't be true. "No, I think that's the cave ceiling."

"Is it me, or is the cave ceiling moving?" Sean asked.

Sean was right. The tiny points of light began to move. The ceiling separated into sparkling fragments. Then the lights stopped in midair, spreading out into a glowing, fluttering mass. Sean was the first to realize what they were.

"They're . . . birds." He almost couldn't believe it. How could birds be living so deep underground?

Thousands of birds hovered above them now, flapping their wings and glowing like fireflies.

"Electric birds?" Sean asked.

"They're like tiny archaeopteryx, birds from the Jurassic period," Trevor said, searching for explanations once again. "But they're bioluminescent, like fireflies, or glowworms."

One of the birds swooped down and hovered near them, curious.

"Cool," Sean said. "Glowbirds."

"You've seen these creatures before?" Hannah asked.

"Just in a museum, as fossils," Trevor said. "These birds have been extinct for . . . roughly a hundred and fifty million years."

Sean held out his hand to the bird. It moved in closer and gave a little chirp. Sean smiled, mesmerized.

Suddenly, there was a loud *whoosh* as the flock of birds shot straight up and flew off in a glowing mass, disappearing through an opening in the cave. It looked like light was streaming in from the other side.

Sean, Hannah, and Trevor ran after them, drawn like moths to the light. They stepped through the entrance, then froze in shock and disbelief.

The birds had led them to a huge underground landscape. A breathtaking waterfall flowed down a cliff covered with bright green grass. On the ground, ferns as tall as pine trees swayed above giant flowers in bright, blinding, neon colors. In the distance, mountains rose up into a strangely glowing, gas-filled, electric sky.

"Where are we?" Sean asked, breathless.

"This . . . this cannot be," Hannah said, her eyes filling with tears.

Trevor stepped forward and opened his arms wide, a crazy grin on his face. "Ladies and gentlemen, I give you . . . the center of the Earth!"

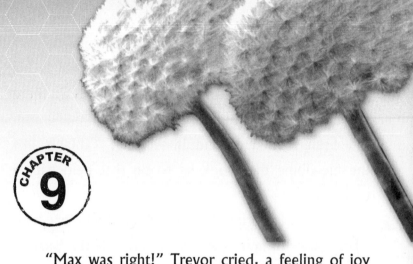

"Max was right!" Trevor cried, a feeling of joy overwhelming him. "Sean! He knew! He nailed it! Your father was right!"

Sean was stunned. He turned to Hannah. "*Your* father was right, too."

Hannah looked completely overwhelmed. Any trace of her calm, composed exterior had vanished.

"They both believed in something that everyone told them was impossible," Trevor said.

"All these years I doubted my father and his ravings," Hannah said, her voice just above a whisper. "But *I* was the fool. He was not crazy."

They soaked in the moment, taking in all there was to see around them. Sean pointed up at the bright sky.

"What's that light?" he asked.

"It's some kind of luminescent gas combination," Trevor said. Thoughts were coming together in his mind like puzzle pieces. "And I'm breathing. So there must be some kind of oxygen."

Sean looked around in wonder. "This is like the bio-dome they took us to on that field trip, a terr . . ."

". . . Terrarium," Trevor finished for him. "Thousands of miles beneath the crust of the Earth."

Hannah had not moved an inch since they'd entered the underground world. She was still completely in shock. "What if . . . what if I'm a Vernian?" she wondered out loud.

Trevor grinned. "You'll get used to it."

There was a rough path in front of them, through the grass, that led behind the waterfall. Trevor led the way this time. The importance of the discovery they'd made was starting to sink in, and it gave him new confidence.

Patches of a slippery, low-growing plant that looked like green moss made the pathway slick. Trevor was taking everything in like a sponge. He checked a thermometer hanging off of Hannah's pack.

"Look at this—it's eighty-two degrees down

here!" he marveled. "This is amazing! Everything's just like Jules Verne described it."

Hannah was trying to make sense of it all. *Journey to the Center of the Earth* was written like a work of fiction, with fictional characters—or was it?

"So Lidenbrock, from the book, was real?" she asked.

"Maybe Lidenbrock got out and told Verne," Trevor guessed.

"He got out?" Sean said. "Now that's the best news I've heard all day."

"If this place exists, biospheres like this, they could exist anywhere on our planet," Trevor said, his mind racing. "It puts into question all the scientific assumptions about the formation of the Earth. Doesn't this just blow your mind?"

"My mind is blown. Yes," Hannah agreed. "But we still need a plan to escape, Trevor."

Trevor knew she was right. A bad thought was forming in the back of his mind. If Lidenbrock had escaped, there was some hope for them. But Max . . . what had happened to Max?

He pushed the thought aside. As a scientist, he knew knowledge was the key to answering more questions. The more he knew about this strange place, the better chance they'd have of getting out.

Sean was amazed by the weird sights all around them. Dandelions as high as his waist were growing on the side of the path. He plucked one and blew on the fluffy seedlings. They danced away through the air.

Trevor began quoting Jules Verne. "The word *cavern* does not convey any idea of this immense space; words . . . are inadequate to describe the discoveries of him who ventures into the deep abysses of Earth."

"Does it say anything in that book about taking a break?" Sean asked. "I'm so hungry."

Hannah snapped back into mountain-guide mode. "Let's rest up ahead at those trees," she suggested. "We can divide one of my protein bars and figure out what we're going to do."

"Protein. Yes. Please," Sean said, feeling suddenly more ravenous than before.

They headed for the trees. Trevor squinted.

"Wait a second," he said. "Those aren't trees."

He was right. The thick brown trunks growing

from the ground weren't tree trunks—they were mushroom stalks. There were no branches or leaves at the top, but giant mushroom caps fifty feet above them.

"I think they're fossilized mushrooms," Trevor said.

"I think you mean *huge* fossilized mushrooms," Sean corrected him. He ran ahead.

Trevor started after him, but Hannah held him back.

"If it's all true, does that mean that everything in the book is real?" she whispered.

"It probably does," Trevor said. Their eyes met.

"Even the really scary parts, with danger lurking around every corner?" Hannah asked.

"I was thinking about those parts, too," Trevor admitted.

Suddenly, the ground rumbled beneath them. Sean's startled cry came through the mushroom forest.

"Trevor! Come quick!" he yelled.

Trevor burst into a run. "Sean! Where are you?"

He found Sean standing motionless in the middle

of a clearing in front of one of the giant mushroom stalks.

"Somebody . . . actually . . . lived here?" Sean asked, unbelieving.

Trevor looked over his shoulder. Someone had carved a crude doorway into the mushroom stalk. Inside, a staircase led up the stem, into the mushroom's fossilized cap.

Sean and Trevor walked up the stairs in silence. It was dark inside the mushroom, but Trevor saw an old kerosene lamp hanging on the wall. He lit it, and yellow light illuminated the room. Someone had used the mushroom as a makeshift shelter. There was expedition gear strewn about, but it looked old—at least a hundred years old.

"This place must have been Lidenbrock's," Trevor said.

Sean began to search the room. There were stacks of old paper piled up on a crudely made desk. The paper looked homemade, as though it had been made from dried leaves. Sean rifled through the sheets and found a leather-bound journal underneath. He picked it up and flipped through it. It was filled with scientific notations, calculations, and hand-drawn maps.

"I think I found Lidenbrock's notebook!" he cried.

Trevor was doing some searching, too. There was a handmade bed in the corner. On top of a pillow made of leaves he spotted a familiar object—a yo-yo crudely carved from wood, fitted with a frayed shoelace. He slipped it into his pocket. That bad feeling he'd had about Max was getting stronger. He walked over to Sean and examined the notebook.

"This was Lidenbrock's shelter, but the writing isn't Lidenbrock's," he said. Now he knew for sure. His brother had been here, all right. So why hadn't he come home?

He put his copy of *Journey to the Center of the Earth* next to the journal. Sean saw he was right—the writing was exactly the same. "This is my father's writing," he said softly.

"Trevor?" Hannah stood in the doorway, her face pale. "I need to talk to you. Outside."

Hannah had followed Trevor when she'd heard Sean call. But something had caught her eye on the way—a strange, uprooted tree. Its roots were covered with rainbow-colored moss. She'd drawn closer to get a better look, and had seen something that she hadn't wanted to see—a skeleton, dressed in modern clothes. She knew it could only mean one thing.

Trevor ran to the site and confirmed what Hannah had guessed. It was Max. His brother hadn't made it out alive. All thoughts of exploring or escape were put aside as they told Sean the news. There was a beach just beyond the mushroom grove, and an ocean glowing with phosphorescent light. Trevor and Hannah dug a hole in the sand, and they buried Max there. Sean and Trevor placed stones on the mound.

Hannah put her hand on Sean's shoulder. "I'm so sorry, Sean."

Sean wasn't sure what to feel. He had been so young when his dad disappeared that he'd never had any hope of finding him alive. Knowing the truth was hard, but it brought him some peace, too, somehow.

"I never had a chance to know him," he said, his voice breaking. "I mean, I wish I had . . ."

He looked up at his uncle. Trevor hung his head

in respect. "I have so much to say about the kind of man Max was," he said. "He was my mentor and my best friend. But I want to read his words from his journal today."

Trevor took the journal from his pocket. "August fourteenth, 1997. I thought I could surprise Trevor and the rest of the world with my discovery, but I've been stuck down here for six weeks. I miss my wife, my brother, and I miss my baby boy. If I don't make it out, I will have lost out on the greatest discovery of them all. That is seeing the man my son would grow up to become."

Sean and Trevor looked at each other.

"You would have loved him, Sean," Trevor said softly. "And he would have been proud of you." He handed Sean the journal.

"Good-bye, Max," Trevor said.

They went back to the mushroom house to rest and plan. Sean quickly fell asleep on a hammock strung up in the corner. Trevor combed through the journal, looking for clues.

"According to Max's journal, the average temperature is usually low," Trevor said. "In the range of seventy-five degrees."

"But it's nearly ten degrees hotter," Hannah pointed out.

Trevor pointed to a diagram Max had drawn. "Look at these maps," he told Hannah. "We're here, in this outer core. This giant air pocket we're in is surrounded by lava. And during cycles of intense seismic activity . . ."

As if on cue, a small tremor interrupted him and shook the ground again.

". . . magma deposits under us build up and they get very, very hot," Trevor explained. "That turns this giant air pocket into an oven."

"Is that what happened to my father?"

Sean sat up on the hammock. He'd been listening the whole time. "I know you think I'm just a kid, but I can handle this. Really."

Trevor saw an expression on Sean's face that he hadn't before. It reminded him of Max.

"Your father was planning to escape, but he ran out of time," Trevor answered honestly. "If Max's notes are right, and they usually are, the temperature down here could easily hit two hundred degrees."

"We'll boil," Hannah said simply.

"So, what do we do?" Sean asked.

Trevor flipped to another page in the journal. A crude drawing showed a network of vents and tubes that led back to the surface.

"We follow Max's escape plan," Trevor said. "He had mapped out a fair amount to the north of here. He must have made some kind of expedition, maybe on a raft or—"

Hannah interrupted him. "With all due respect, Max didn't make it. Should we really be following his plan?"

"Yes!" Sean said firmly. He jumped off of the hammock and faced Trevor and Hannah.

"My father was right about how to get down here," Sean said. "And he was right about getting back up!"

Trevor looked at Sean and nodded. Sean was right. Max might not have made it, but his notes would help them escape.

"According to the map, on the other side of the ocean, directly north, Max spotted a series of small rivers," Trevor continued. "These rivers could flow toward geyser holes that could lead us all the way to the surface."

"So?" Hannah asked.

"So, if we could get on one of those rivers, we could take it to the geyser, and hitch a ride all the way topside," Trevor replied.

"Sounds like a plan," Sean said. "I like topside."

"The tricky part is we have to get there before the water gets too hot and starts to evaporate," Trevor said. "Once everything goes dry down here, there's no way out."

Sean checked one of the thermometers.

"It's ninety-five degrees," he reported.

Trevor frowned. "When we got here it was eighty-two. It's going up fast."

"How much time do you think we have?" Hannah asked.

"Thirty-six, maybe forty-eight hours," he said. He opened the journal to another sketch of Max's: a design for a sail-powered raft.

They got to work on the raft right away. The air seemed to grow more humid and hot each minute. Trevor and Sean gathered long, flexible reeds from a patch near the water. Hannah bound them together to form the floor of the raft.

"How are we doing?" Trevor asked, dumping another pile of reeds at her feet.

"Good, but it's almost one hundred degrees," she replied, wiping the sweat from her forehead. Her voice was solemn. The hotter it got, the less time they had.

They worked as quickly as they could, and they used whatever materials they had. Hannah made a sail from Lidenbrock's old sheets and tarps. Trevor made two small masts out of stiff reeds, but decided they didn't need a main mast. Instead, the sails would fly above the raft, attached by a rope—almost like a huge kite.

Trevor carved a rudder out of a fossilized mushroom. While they worked, they ate fruit gathered in the forest, and Hannah filled a water bottle with fresh water from the stream.

Hours later, Trevor and Sean attached the rudder to the finished raft.

"Nice work," Trevor said. "How's that feel?"

Sean tugged on the mast. "Feels solid."

Trevor took something out of his pocket. He'd found it with Max's belongings—a metal compass pocked with scratch marks. Now he handed it to Sean.

"It was your dad's," he said.

"Wow," Sean said, taking it from him. "Thanks, Uncle Trevor."

"I remember the Christmas your mom gave this to him," Trevor told Sean. "She said it was so he could always find a way home. Maybe this will get you back to her."

Sean studied the compass. "I do have a memory of him," he said. He'd never thought of it until now. "He showed me how it worked. I'd hold it out, and he'd twirl me around, and we'd watch the needle spin."

"Now it's yours, but you've got to remember something," Trevor said. "Down here, the polarity is reversed. So north is south and south is north. We have to sail north across this sea."

"You mean south," Sean said.

"Exactly."

Sean smiled. He was feeling a lot of different emotions right now. He looked out at the sea.

Trevor gave Sean a moment to deal with his thoughts. He and Hannah packed the raft with their provisions and equipment, and they prepared to set sail.

Sean looked at the sails that lay limply on the sand. "I don't think it's going to catch the wind."

"Just wait for the gust," Trevor said, letting out the rope lines a bit.

They waited. And waited some more. They were about to give up hope when a strong breeze whipped through the trees behind them.

"Okay, now!" Trevor cried.

The three of them hurled the sails into the air. The wind pushed against them, and they billowed out against the neon sky. They pushed the raft into the water and quickly jumped on.

Whoosh! The kite-like sails flapped high above them, easily pulling the raft across the water. Trevor worked the rudder, steering the ship as best as he could.

Sean noticed a small, neon-blue dot fly toward them across the sky. It was the little glowbird he'd seen in the grotto.

"He's back," Sean said happily. "Hey, little guy."

But the smooth sailing didn't last long. The winds were picking up, the waves were beginning to swell, and dark clouds were forming on the horizon—sure signs of a storm.

"Are you seeing those clouds?" Hannah asked. Trevor nodded. "The current's pulling us in the direction we want to go. Maybe we should lower the kite?"

"No," Trevor said. "We're up to a hundred and fourteen degrees. We need all the speed we can get."

Hannah pulled on the rope, tightening the wildly flapping sail. Now they were moving even faster. Trevor smiled at her.

"That's the Icelandic spirit!"

The storm clouds quickly gathered across the sky. The winds kicked up even more, and soon sheets of warm rain began to pour from the sky. Sean huddled under an extra tarp for shelter while Hannah and Trevor manned the sails and the rudder.

"Just a little storm! No big deal!" Trevor called out.

Hannah grinned. "That's the American spirit!"

The rain finally started to slow down, but the winds were picking up even faster. Soon it would be difficult to control the raft. Trevor could tell that everyone's hopes were fading.

"Hey, Sean, enough adventure for you yet?" he asked, trying to pick up his spirits.

"I'm good, thanks," Sean said listlessly.

Then Hannah pointed at the water.

"Something's moving down there," she said. In the distance, some neon shapes were darting under the waves.

"It's nothing," Trevor said. "Probably just

bioluminescent plankton."

But as the shapes grew closer, they grew larger, too.

"They look pretty big for plankton," Sean pointed out. "I think they're some kind of fish."

Sean got on his knees for a closer look. "Sean, back up," Trevor warned. "We're not at Sea World—"

As he spoke, a big, prehistoric fish burst out of the water just inches from Sean's face. Its big, gaping mouth held rows of razor-like teeth. Sean shrieked and quickly ducked, and the fish splashed back into the water.

Before anyone could react, a second fish leaped up, right in Trevor's face! He fell back, throwing his arms out to block it, but ended up grabbing it instead. Its hideous jaws snapped just inches from his face.

"Agh! Get off!" Trevor screamed. He threw the fish into the water.

"In the book, these fish are referred to as a species of ancient Pterichthys," he said.

Trevor's eyes scanned the sea as he caught his breath. The glow-in-the-dark fish were swarming around the raft. More fish were joining them every second.

"What else does the book say?" Sean asked nervously.

"It says there are a lot of them!" Hannah replied.

Five fish jumped out of the water at once, arching over the raft and wildly snapping their teeth.

"They're everywhere!" Sean screamed, flailing his arms.

Trevor thought quickly. He tossed one of the oars to Sean with a cry of "Batter up!"

Sean jumped to his feet. "Right," he said. Another fish flew out of the water, and he swung the oar. *Whack!* The unlucky fish went flying back over the waves.

"Line drive!" Sean cheered.

Out of nowhere, a strange musical sound carried through the roar of the wind.

"Do you hear something?" Hannah asked.

Sean couldn't believe it. "It's my cell!" He took the phone from his pocket and quickly picked it up. "Hello? Hello?"

"Sean?" asked the voice on the other end. "It's Mom."

"Mom, can you hear me?" Sean shouted.

"I think we have a bad connection," Elizabeth said. "Can you hear me now? Where are you?"

Sean knew he couldn't begin to tell his mom the truth. "Trevor and I, we're on, um, a fishing trip," he began. It wasn't *exactly* a lie.

Another fish flew up on the boat, and Trevor grabbed it by the tail.

"Wow, Uncle Trevor just caught a big one," Sean said.

"Are you having—"

Wham! Another fish jumped up, knocking the phone from Sean's hand and into the water.

"My phone!" Sean yelled.

"Sean! Here's an easy one!" Trevor had grabbed the fish. Now he tossed it over to Sean. *Whack!* The flesh-eating fish flew back into the sea.

"Out of the ballpark!" he cried.

Then his smile faded. A huge creature erupted from the depths of the sea, hungry for the flying fish. It looked like a sea serpent Sean had seen in a movie once. Its eyes were an evil shade of yellow, and each one was as big as Sean's head. Huge, jagged teeth jutted out from its mouth.

"*Aaaaaaaah!* What's that?" Sean screamed. He

stood, frozen in fear, as a fish jumped across the water, fleeing the sea monster. It was headed right for Sean! The fish was inches away from his face now . . .

Snap! The creature's huge jaws shut, and it gulped down the fish.

"It doesn't want us," Trevor realized. "It wants the fish."

"Are you sure about that?" Hannah asked.

"Well, I'm more hopeful than sure," Trevor admitted.

To their horror, three more sea serpents broke the surface, attracted by the glowing fish.

"We have to get out of their way," Trevor said urgently.

Lightning flashed across the sky. The sea serpents were violently churning the water, and the raft rocked up and down. One of the monsters crashed into one of the small masts, loosening the rope line. Trevor grabbed it just in time.

"Hannah, grab the other line!" Trevor yelled. "Keep the sail up!"

Hannah dove for the other line and pulled with all her might. Sean took Trevor's place at the rudder.

The sail caught a violent blast of wind, jerking the craft off course.

"It's pulling too hard!" Hannah shouted. "It's too strong!"

"Sean, steer away!" Trevor told them.

Sean aimed the raft away from the pod of sea serpents. The raft slowly changed its course.

"It's working!" Sean said. "You're the man, Uncle Trev."

"Yeah, that's what I've been telling the scientific community for years," Trevor joked.

They all felt a sense of relief. But it didn't last long. A huge gust of wind suddenly filled the kite, yanking the rope line through Hannah's hands. She cried out as the rope ripped the skin from her palms. She fell back, her hands bruised and raw.

"Hannah!" Trevor rushed to her side, wrapping her hands in a cloth.

That left both lines unmanned. Sean noticed it first. Hannah's rope line was starting to pull loose, and the sail was deflating quickly.

"I got it!" Sean said, leaving his post at the rudder. He wrapped Hannah's line around his wrist.

Then the damaged mast began to fail, and the

other rope line was coming loose. Sean reached across the raft to grab it, still holding on to Hannah's line.

"Sean . . . no!" Trevor warned.

It all happened so fast. Trevor bolted to stop Sean, but Sean had already grabbed the second mast and started wrapping the line around his arm. Before Trevor could reach him, another wicked wind whipped up, tearing the mast from the raft.

"Sean, let it go!" Trevor yelled.

It was no use. The powerful wind yanked Sean off of the ship with the mast. Trevor dove to catch him but missed, and Sean shot skyward into the gale.

"Help! Trevor, help me!" Sean screamed, struggling to free himself from the rope.

"No! Sean!" Trevor yelled.

But it was too late.

Trevor and Hannah watched helplessly as the wind carried Sean away and out of sight. Without sails, there was no way they could chase after him.

The wind churned up the waves, carrying the raft toward the nearby shore. Trevor and Hannah hung on tightly. The raft splintered as it crashed into the rocky coast, but they were unhurt.

They walked away from the raft, scanning the dense green jungle for any sign of Sean.

"Sean!" Hannah called out.

"Can you hear us?" Trevor yelled.

Hannah sighed. "The wind could have taken him anywhere."

"No, he's here somewhere, and I'm not leaving this place without him," Trevor said firmly. "He's—"

Hannah looked deep into Trevor's eyes. "He's

your nephew. I understand."

"Yeah," Trevor nodded. "He's my family."

From the depths of the jungle, a distant roar reached their ears. They eyed each other.

"Are we going to pretend we just didn't hear that?" Hannah asked.

"I think that's best," Trevor agreed.

Hannah nodded toward a low cliff overlooking the sea. "We'll see more from that rise up there."

They began the hike through the jungle. Trevor knew time was running out. Sean might have drowned in the sea, or been swallowed by one of those horrible sea monsters. But he couldn't think about that. He couldn't give up hope. He'd already lost Max to this Vernian nightmare.

He wasn't going to lose Sean, too.

Trevor and Hannah took a rest in the middle of their trek to the cliff. Trevor grabbed Hannah's pack and began to empty it out.

"What are you doing?" Hannah asked.

"If we're going to find Sean, we have to move quickly," Trevor explained. "I'm going to take out anything we don't need. You know, lighten the load."

Hannah took her water bottle from Trevor, finishing off the last few drops so she could get rid of it. That's when Trevor noticed a giant Venus flytrap–like plant looming ominously behind her, slowly opening its large mouth-like leaves . . .

"Duck!" yelled Trevor. Hannah reacted just in time, swiftly dodging the plant as it unsuccessfully tried to swallow her whole. Trevor grabbed Hannah's walking stick and—*THWACK!*—decapitated the frightening plant in a single blow. Then he grabbed Hannah, and together, they raced out of harm's way as a group of giant Venus flytraps closed in on them.

"You okay?" Hannah asked.

"Yeah," Trevor said, breathing heavily. "So much for taking a rest. Now, let's make our way up to that cliff so we can find Sean."

Sean slowly came back to consciousness. He could feel that he was facedown in the sand. He was dazed, but nothing hurt. That was a good sign. He groggily opened his eyes.

"Aaahh!"

A fish stared back at him, its jaws open wide. It took a second for Sean to realize it was dead. Startled, he sat up and tried to take stock of his surroundings.

His backpack, drenched with seawater, was on the sand next to him. The rope lines were wrapped around his body, and the bedraggled sail was draped over some rocks on the shore.

"Hello! Trevor? Hannah?"

There was no reply. His mouth was cracked and dry, and the heat was unbearable. Without thinking, he reached for a nearby seashell filled with water and took a sip.

"Blech!" He spat out the hot, salty water. He knew enough about survival to know that drinking saltwater was a sure way to die. Exhausted, he stood up and wiped the sweat from his brow.

"Okay, remember the plan," he told himself. "Gotta head north and find those rivers. That's where they're located."

From the corner of his eye, Sean saw a small light. He turned to see the glowbird hovering next to him.

"Hey, little guy," Sean said. He was relieved to see a familiar face—even if it did have a beak. "Where are we?"

The glowbird began to chirp excitedly. Sean laughed. "Sorry, I don't speak Jurassic."

The bird seemed to understand. It turned and flew away from the shore. Then it stopped, hovering, and looked back at Sean.

"Follow you? Is that what you're saying?" Sean asked. "Do you know where I can find some water?"

Sean stopped. "How desperate am I to be talking to a bird? I must be losing it."

He shook his head and followed the bird across the landscape. They walked up a rocky ridge. The uphill climb was extra difficult in the extreme heat. Sean began to wonder if he had made a huge mistake.

The bird led him around a bend, then stopped, hovering. Sean could hardly believe his eyes. A trickle of clear water ran down a rock, into a stream.

"Water? Is it real?" Sean asked.

He dropped to his knees to drink. To his relief, he found that the water was fresh. Satisfied, he sat down and took his father's compass out of his pocket. The arrow was pointing due south.

"South. Good," he said. "The river's due north. That's where I'm going."

The bird gave a little chirp and urged him onward.

Sean's tired legs ached as he made his way up the trail. He noticed that the stones on the path seemed to be getting larger.

Suddenly, he tripped. He crashed down on top of the rocks, and his pocketknife flew out of his pocket.

Sean gasped. The knife didn't land. It floated in the air, inches above the ground. For a moment, he stared, dazed. He looked at the floating pocketknife, then at the compass in his hand. The compass needle and the knife were both pointing in the same direction.

"Oh, I get it," he realized. "It's a magnetic field."

He grabbed the knife and stuck it back in his pocket. Then he began to run down the path. The stones underneath his feet seemed to push down with each step, then bob back into place. Sean looked down, then froze.

The rock he was standing on was floating, just like the pocketknife.

"No way," Sean said, steadying himself. "Magnetic rocks."

He was floating a few inches off the ground, but just ahead, the ridge came to an end. It dropped off into a deep canyon. Sean guessed the drop down was at least one hundred feet. The glowbird waited for him on the other side, and there was only one way across.

Large, flat stones stretched out in front of him, making a floating path to the opposite side of the canyon. Each massive stone looked sturdy enough, but Sean could see they weren't perfectly steady. Each rock swayed slowly in the breeze, and floated at a slightly different level.

Sean took a deep breath. He had to go north. That was the way out. To do that, he'd have to cross the canyon—but he'd have to do it carefully.

One false step, and he'd plummet to the bottom of the canyon. His journey would be over for good.

Sean tried to steel his nerves. The glowbird gave an encouraging chirp from the other side.

He tentatively reached out a foot to the next stone and put some weight on it. It sunk slightly, but he could feel the steady pull underneath, keeping it afloat. He stepped on it completely, and it dipped suddenly. He gasped, steadying himself.

So far, so good. The next stone floated a few feet in front of him. Too far to step. He'd have to jump.

Grimacing, Sean launched himself and landed firmly on the next stone. Thankfully, the stones were big enough to make easy targets. His confidence up, he jumped to the next stone, then the next. But the stones were floating farther and farther apart as he made his way. He jumped again, and this time he barely made it, landing on all fours.

Sean grunted and got to his knees. The momentum of his landing had caused the stone to move forward, knocking into the next stone. It slowly floated away, out of reach.

Sean's heart began a panicked drumbeat. He looked behind him, but the stones had all floated away. He had to go forward, but the leap to the next stone looked really far.

Sean closed his eyes, steadying himself. He got a running start, then leaped across the chasm. His feet landed on the back edge of the stone. He'd barely made it.

But his relief didn't last long. All of his weight was on the back of the stone, which began to tilt backward. Sean reached out and grabbed the edges of the stone with both arms just in time. He held on with all his might as the stone began to turn upside down.

"Whoaaaaa!" Sean yelled.

His headlamp fell out of his pocket and dropped into the abyss below. Sean held his breath as the stone rotated back around, putting him right-side up again. But before he could release his grip, the stone tilted once more. He closed his eyes in sheer terror.

The stone righted itself once again, and finally

leveled off. Sean opened his eyes. The solid edge of the canyon was just inches away. He gratefully crawled off of the magnetic rock onto solid land, gasping for breath.

He stood up and followed the glowbird once again.

From the top of the rise, Trevor and Hannah could see a flat plain stretched out before them. At the opposite end, a river glimmered in the light.

"There's our way out," Trevor said.

"Trevor, it's over a hundred and twenty degrees," Hannah said, her voice anxious. "Time is running out . . . for all of us . . ."

Trevor thought for a moment. "You should go, Hannah," he said finally. "Get to that river and find something, anything you can use to carry you to the surface."

Hannah was startled. "What? I can't leave you and Sean."

Trevor pointed to the river, where a cloud of steam was rising.

"Water's already starting to evaporate," he said. "Who knows how long we have? Please go. You need to save yourself."

"Don't be crazy," Hannah said.

"I promised I'd take care of Sean, and that's what I'm going to do," Trevor said. "Now go."

Hannah shook her head. "I can't! Not without you." Tears shone in her blue eyes.

"This was all my fault," Trevor said sadly. "He's my responsibility. Now you have to get out of here while you still can."

Hannah looked into his eyes. Then she suddenly leaned forward, kissing him.

Trevor was stunned. "What was that?"

"Just in case," she said.

"Don't worry. We'll be right behind," he promised. Hannah lingered, stunned, while Trevor walked away. "I hope so, Trevor Anderson," she said.

She reluctantly headed toward the river. She knew why Trevor wanted her to go. He didn't want to be responsible for losing her, too.

But it didn't make her feel any better.

She ran toward the river, fueled by determination. She would find a way out—a way out for all of them.

CHAPTER 13

Sean followed the glowbird through a giant crack in the hillside. The bird had been a great guide so far. Sean had high hopes that the river he was looking for was waiting for him on the other side.

He emerged from the crack, shaking the dust off of his clothes, and his hopes faded. A vast desert stretched out in every direction, bordered by canyon walls to the west and east. There was no sign of the river, or any sign of life at all.

"Trevor! Hannah! Where are you?" Sean shouted.

The glowbird flew up ahead, and Sean knew he had no choice but to follow. He wearily stumbled across the blazing desert.

The landscape changed as they moved on, and now huge, white rocks lay in the sand around him.

Sean checked his compass.

"South is north, north is south," he repeated. "If this compass is right, I must be getting close. Right?"

The white rocks seemed to be everywhere now, and Sean had to climb over and around them to follow the glowbird. He scrambled on top of a round boulder and then jumped off on the other side.

His feet hit the dusty ground with a thud. He looked back up at the boulder to see how high he'd jumped.

Then he froze.

A huge eye socket stared back at him. The boulder wasn't a boulder at all—it was an enormous skull with jagged teeth and gaping holes for the eyes and nose. The shape of the skull was unmistakable.

It was a dinosaur.

Sean realized in amazement that the white rocks were actually a huge dinosaur skeleton. He'd seen one in a museum once, but he hadn't been able to touch it. He reached out and touched the smooth bone.

"Wow," he said. He held out his arms and did his best dinosaur imitation. "Roaaaar!"

RooooooAAAAAAR!

Sean spun around, his heart pounding. It hadn't been his imagination. A real roar had echoed through the canyon, and a terrifying thought overtook him. Where there were dinosaur skeletons, there were bound to be dinosaurs.

He scanned the area for a place to hide. The sound of huge footsteps thundered in the distance, and he knew they were getting closer. Finally he spotted a rock outcropping jutting out from the canyon. He ran to it, pressing his body close.

The Earth shook underneath Sean's feet as the footsteps got closer. Suddenly, the rumblings stopped. Sean held his breath, waiting.

Slowly, slowly, he leaned over and peeked around the rock. There was nothing in sight. He stayed frozen in place, only daring to move his eyes.

Something fell from the sky, past his face. He looked down to see a huge glob of spit next to his shoe. His heart pounded in his chest, and he slowly looked up.

A gigantic dinosaur stared down at him. Its scaly skin was a mottled, pale white color. Razor-edged teeth, each one as big as Sean, snapped in its massive mouth.

The giant reptile lunged. Sean ran, terrified, faster than he'd ever run in his life. He spotted a small opening in the canyon wall and headed for it. The dinosaur's huge claw smashed into the ground beside him.

Sean propelled forward as though he had rockets on his feet. The dinosaur stomped behind him, getting closer with each step.

"Aaaaaaaah!" Sean screamed.

The dinosaur dove down, and Sean could feel its hot breath on his neck. He dove for the hole, tucking his arms and legs under him. Then he rolled inside. He sat, breathing heavily for a moment.

Then, suddenly, the dinosaur's head burst through the opening in the canyon. Sean scrambled to the opposite wall, flattening himself against the rocks as the beast grunted, trying to push its head farther into the crevice. There was no way out.

"Help! Help!" he screamed.

Fear coursed through his body as the monster pushed its head closer. The sharp, yellow teeth were just inches from his face now. He closed his eyes. His heart beat wildly as he waited for the worst.

Suddenly, the stones behind him gave way, and

Sean fell back.

"Sean!"

Trevor's face appeared behind him, through the hole in the rocks.

"Trevor! Get me out! Hurry!" Sean pleaded.

Trevor yanked away a few more stones and pulled Sean through the hole. Sean gave his uncle a grateful hug.

"Sean, I am so glad to see you," Trevor said.

"Yeah, me too," Sean answered.

The ground began to shake. The dinosaur's snout pounded through the narrow opening, sending rocks flying all around them. Trevor and Sean scrambled to dodge the debris. Trevor grabbed Sean's shirt and they stumbled down a slope, away from the ever-widening hole in the wall. Chunks of rock bounced down the hill all around them.

Trevor glanced over his shoulder to see the dinosaur still pounding away. It wasn't free yet, but it would be soon.

"What is that?" Trevor asked as they ran.

"Haven't you ever seen a giant albino dinosaur before?" Sean asked, panting.

Trevor smiled in spite of the danger they were in.

"Not so up close and personal."

They skidded to a stop at the bottom of the hill. Sean saw a distant geyser of steam across the plain.

"Is that the river out there?" he asked.

Trevor nodded. "Yeah, let's go."

They charged ahead. Trevor looked back to see the dinosaur blast through the wall and leap down the hill toward them.

"Where's Hannah?" Sean asked as they ran.

"Hopefully on her way out already," Trevor replied.

Sean looked back over his shoulder. "He's too fast! We won't make it!"

Trevor scanned the surroundings, looking for some kind of shelter, some kind of escape. Suddenly, his eyes widened. The surface of the plain was glassy and mottled.

"It's the stuff we fell through," Trevor said, stopping. "The muscovite. It can't possibly hold him."

"Yeah, but it might not hold *you*, either," Sean said. He knew what his uncle wanted to do. He'd risk his own life to lure the dinosaur onto the muscovite.

But Trevor had a plan. "You keep running toward the river," he instructed. He ran away from Sean and picked up a rock. He threw it at the beast to get its attention.

"Trevor, no!" Sean cried. He felt like he had just discovered his uncle. He didn't want to lose him now.

"Go, Sean, go!" Trevor urged. "Get to the river!"

Sean knew he couldn't stop Trevor. He took off, running on the edge of the plain, avoiding the muscovite.

He glanced back. The dinosaur was charging at Trevor!

Trevor raced across the muscovite plain with the dinosaur in hot pursuit. Sean ran a parallel track on the edge of the plain. The monstrous beast roared as it bore down on Trevor.

"Trevor, he's gaining on you!" Sean screamed.

Trevor's heart pounded as he pushed himself to go faster. "Come on, come on!" he yelled down at the muscovite. "Crack!"

Then there was a splintering sound as thin cracks formed in the muscovite with each step of the dinosaur. The cracks were snaking out toward Trevor, too, and chunks of muscovite were falling into the abyss below them.

Trevor dared a glance behind him. A huge crack filled the air as the muscovite broke into pieces under the dinosaur's feet. The beast let out an ear-splitting shriek as it began to fall through the floor of the plain.

There were huge holes all around them now. The floor buckled under Trevor's feet. He saw a huge hole in the muscovite in front of him. He ran for the edge and then jumped with all his might.

"Aaaaaaaah!" He shrieked as he fell into the hole, missing the other side. Behind him, the dinosaur plummeted into the abyss.

Sean watched the scene in horror. "Uncle Trevor!" he screamed.

He ran to the edge of the ledge, his heart in his throat. To his amazement, he saw Trevor pulling himself up over the edge of the hole, gasping for breath.

"Don't try that at home, Sean," he said, collapsing back on the muscovite.

Sean was pale and shaking. "Trevor . . . that was, like . . . and you were, like . . ."

A huge tremor shook them both, and more of the muscovite fell down into the hole.

"Let's go," he said.

They quickly got to the safe edge of the plain and headed for a cave with steam escaping from the entrance. Where there was steam, there was water.

A blanket of steam assaulted them as they walked inside the cave. It took a moment for their eyes to adjust to the darkness. Through the steam, they could see a river bubbling and boiling in front of them.

"The river!" Sean cried, but his happiness faded. "How are we going to get to the geyser? The water is boiling."

Trevor looked around frantically. "We need a boat. I don't know, a log maybe. Anything that floats."

Sean scanned the horizon, but all he could see was the steam and bubbling water. He turned the other way and saw a figure moving up the river, through the fog.

It was Hannah, floating toward them in an upside-down dinosaur skull the size of a party boat.

"You didn't think I was going to leave without you! Get in!" she ordered them.

Sean was awestruck. "She's the greatest mountain guide on the planet."

There was no way to stop the skull, so Trevor and Sean had to jump from the riverbank into the moving boat. They landed with a thud on the thick floor. Trevor looked up at Hannah's smiling face.

"I'm definitely charging you extra for this part," she joked.

Trevor smiled. "And you're worth every last krona."

They floated down the river inside a tunnel. From the growing heat, they guessed the river was taking them down to the bottom of a volcano. If Max's plans were right, there would be a geyser on the bottom, one that would shoot them back to the surface.

"How hot is it now?" Sean wondered. He'd never been so hot in his life.

"I don't know," Trevor said, panting. "The thermometer tops out at a hundred twenty-five."

Suddenly, they felt a bump on the bottom of the skull boat.

"What was that?" Sean asked.

"It's the bottom of the river!" Trevor realized. "It's getting shallow. We're running out of water."

Trevor turned on a flashlight. This was good news. They might be getting closer to the bottom of the volcano—and the geyser they needed to propel them back to the surface.

"Hang on!" Trevor told them. "The ride might get a bit—"

"*AAAAAHHHH!*" All three travelers screamed as the skull plunged down a deep drop.

Wham! The skull landed, and they grunted as the impact sent them tumbling to the skull floor.

"Everybody okay?" Trevor asking, rising to his feet.

Sean and Hannah stood, nodding.

"Where are we?" Sean wondered.

Hannah looked over the edge of the boat and pointed down. The skull boat was lodged in the cracks of the craggy rock walls. There was a drop beneath them, and a bright orange spot of light glowed there.

"What's that light down there?" Sean asked.

"Magma," Trevor answered. "Lava. And it's rising."

The orange spot grew even as Trevor spoke.

"I thought there was supposed to be water in here," Sean said, panicking. "Water shooting in the tunnel!"

"We're too late," Trevor realized. "We missed the geyser."

Sean paced the floor of the boat. "What do we do, Trevor?"

Trevor was too deep in thought to reply. Hannah rummaged inside her bag and pulled out a length of rope.

"We could climb back up where we came from, to that dry riverbed," she suggested.

"And sit there waiting to get baked?" Sean snapped.

"Or we can sit here and wait for the boiling lava," she answered. She eyed Trevor. "Hey, you're supposed to chime in with a big idea now, Professor."

"I'm trying to think of a big idea," he told her. "Without water, there's no steam. Without steam, we're not going anywhere. It doesn't look like there's been any water in this tunnel for hours."

"But the walls are still wet," Sean pointed out.

"Impossible," Trevor said. "It's at least a hundred and thirty degrees in here."

Hannah pointed. "Look behind you!"

Trevor obeyed and saw they were right. He ran his fingers along the wet wall, thinking. "It's cold."

Sean peered over the edge of the boat. The bubbling lava was rising quickly now.

"Trevor! The lava's getting closer!" he screamed.

But Trevor was deep in thought. How could the water be cold inside a volcano? The answer struck him like a lightning bolt. "There's water behind the wall!"

"What?" Hannah asked.

"Some kind of pocket," Trevor said, speaking quickly. "There must be a heck of a lot of it to still be—"

His voice hushed as he stroked the wall, tracing a vein of minerals in the rock.

"Magnesium," he whispered. "The walls are lined with magnesium."

The ominous orange light of the lava rose up inside the volcano like a terrible sunrise. The rock walls shuddered as a mild earthquake struck, sending small rocks falling from above.

Sean screamed in terror. "We're slipping!" If the skull boat fell, they'd plunge into the boiling hot lava below.

"How many flares you got left, Hannah?" Trevor asked.

Hannah reached into her bag and pulled them out. "Three."

Trevor took the first flare and banged it hard against the floor of the boat. It ignited, and he hurled it at the wall below them, where the vein of magnesium was thickest. The flare hit the wall with a bang and then ricocheted, falling into the burning lava.

Trevor took a deep breath. He lit the second flare, hurled it—and missed the magnesium by a mile.

"Trevor, maybe I should try," Sean suggested.

"Can't take the chance," Trevor said. He grabbed the last flare and leaned over the edge of the skull, headfirst. "Hannah, do you have any rope left?"

Hannah didn't need any instruction. She pulled out a line and tied one end to Trevor's feet, and the other end to the skull. Sean helped Hannah lower Trevor down. He hung there, upside down, following the vein of magnesium with his hands. He needed to find the perfect spot.

He banged the flare on the wall, but it didn't spark. He aimed the light from his headlamp and saw the problem.

"Wet," he said.

Trevor looked down. The lava was shooting up

fast. Trevor turned the flare over and examined the other side. It was dry enough to light. He banged it against the wall, but nothing happened.

Bang! Trevor tried again.

Bang! Again.

He wildly slammed the flare against the wall, willing it to ignite. The lava was almost upon them now. This was their last, and only, hope.

"Trevor, hurry!" Sean gasped. "The air . . . too hot . . . can't breathe!"

Trevor slammed the flare again. A spark lit up! He held it to the magnesium vein, holding his breath.

The magnesium caught fire! Trevor swung back on the rope as white light exploded from the vein.

"Pull me up!" he yelled.

Sean and Hannah yanked at the rope. Exhausted, Sean lost his grip, but Hannah hung on, using all her strength to pull Trevor up to safety.

"Watch the teeth! Watch the teeth!" Trevor warned as the sharp canines jabbed him.

Hannah yanked him over the side. He landed right beside her.

"Who saved who that time?" he said, grinning.

Below them, the magnesium crackled and burned all along the wall.

"Let's call it a draw," Hannah replied. Then . . .

BOOM!

The wet wall exploded, and water burst out like a hundred fire hoses.

"Yes!" Sean cheered.

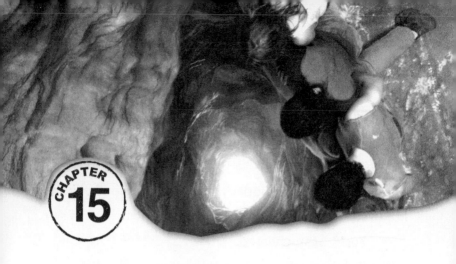

The water cascaded down the tunnel, hitting the boiling, churning lava. A huge cloud of steam formed as hot met cold. It powered up the tunnel right toward them.

"Get back from the edge!" Trevor cried.

All three dove for the thick floor of the skull, holding on to one another. Hannah strapped them into the skull with a rope—just in time.

SHOOOOOOOM!

A geyser of boiling water and steam shot the skull upward through the volcano, away from the center of the Earth. It rocketed faster and faster at breakneck speed.

"This thing's heating up!" Sean cried, worried.

"Hang on!" Trevor called back.

"Trust me," Hannah replied, "I'm hanging on!"

Sean raised his head. A tiny dot of blue shone above them. He pointed. "Look!"

"Is that—sky?" Hannah wondered.

The skull hurtled upward, propelled by the boiling water that rose dangerously closer to the sides of the boat. Trevor, Hannah, and Sean lay flat on the bottom like astronauts facing punishing g-forces. The blue sky loomed larger above them, almost near enough to touch now. Trevor put his arms around Sean and Hannah.

WHOOOSH! The skull blasted out of the volcano, flying through the air, supported by a giant plume of water and steam. They screamed with joy.

They'd made it!

Then the steam dissipated, and the skull began to fall to Earth.

"Hang on, everybody!" Trevor cried.

"Stop saying that!" Hannah said.

BAM! The skull smacked into the side of the volcano, skidding down the slope like an out-of-control bobsled. Sean lifted his head as the skull rocketed toward rows of grapevines at the bottom of the slope.

"Duck!" he yelled.

They plowed through the vines, tearing up row after row. The skull kicked up grapes, leaves, and twigs in its wake.

Sean ventured another look. They were zooming toward a wooden farmhouse! He closed his eyes, certain of disaster. But the vines had slowed down the movement of the boat, and it gradually slowed to a stop, right at the front door.

Hannah loosened the ropes, and they all sat up, dazed and covered in grapes. Trevor looked over his shoulder at the volcano and recognized it immediately. But it couldn't be true.

"Mount Vesuvius?" he said, unbelieving.

"What?" Hannah didn't believe it, either.

Trevor laughed. "Hey, Sean. If your mother asks you what you did this weekend, tell her your uncle took you to Italy."

Sean looked around. "Italy?"

A gray-haired man ran across the fields, angry and distraught. He shouted at them in Italian. Sean didn't know what he was saying, but he had a pretty good idea why he was upset—his vineyard was ruined.

Luckily, Sean also had a pretty good idea how

to make him feel better. He dug in his knapsack and pulled out a huge diamond.

Trevor's mouth fell open. "Sean, you didn't—"

"What?" Sean asked, grinning. "I just took a few geological samples, that's all."

Trevor opened the backpack. It was filled with diamonds!

"Okay, so a few pounds of samples," Sean admitted. "What do you want? I'm the son of a scientist."

He handed the big diamond to the old man, talking slowly. "Here, for you," he said. "Take it. We are sorry."

The old man looked at the jewel, then at Sean. He smiled.

"You want to go down other side of the hill, too?" he asked in English. "Go ahead! Anything you want!"

A few days later, Trevor burst into his lab at the university. Leonard was at his desk, eating a sandwich and surfing the Internet.

"I'm back, Leonard!" Trevor said. "You can stop what you're doing."

"What am I doing?" Leonard asked, a guilty look on his face.

"You're looking for work," Trevor said knowingly. "Stop. You've got a job with the Anderson and Ásgeirsson Institute for Tectonophysical Exploration!"

Leonard stopped typing. "The Anderson and what?"

"I'm still working on the name," Trevor said. "But the point is, we're back in business! And a rising tide lifts all boats!"

"Excellent. I think," Leonard said, mildly confused. "Am I a boat?"

Trevor's archrival Kitzens emerged from Trevor's office, followed by a team of building contractors.

"What are you doing here?" Trevor asked.

"We're just measuring for where the shelves are going to go," he replied, a snide smile on his face. "Where've you been, Anderson? Word is you stood up your Monday lecture."

"I took a quick vacation," Trevor quipped. "Greatest trip of my life."

"Yeah?" Kitzens asked, raising an eyebrow. "Tell me about it."

"You can read about it in October's *Scientific American*, Kitzens," Trevor replied.

Kitzens looked incredulous. *"Scientific American?"*

"That's right," said Trevor, enjoying the moment. "Listen, I just wanted to say no hard feelings about you taking my lab. I really need my own building, anyway."

"Your own building? Yeah?" Kitzens had a smirk on his face. He clearly thought Trevor was lying. "And how is that going to happen, exactly?"

"Oh, I fell into a small fortune," Trevor said casually.

Just then, Hannah walked into the lab, cleaned up from their adventure and looking absolutely gorgeous. "Hello," she said.

"This is Hannah," Trevor said. "She's going to be my partner in the new lab."

Hannah locked her arm through Trevor's. Kitzens was completely stunned.

"Wow," he said. "Um, lucky you, Anderson."

Trevor smiled. "Yeah. Lucky me."

It was the last day of Sean's visit. His bags were packed. Trevor and Hannah walked him out of the apartment.

"So tomorrow you're a Canadian," Hannah remarked.

"Looks that way," Sean said. He sighed a little. He hadn't wanted to visit his uncle at all. Now he didn't want to leave.

Trevor put an arm around Sean. "That wasn't too bad, was it? Our little male bonding time . . . maybe we'll do it for two weeks next time."

"Two weeks?" Sean said hopefully.

"How about Christmas break?" Trevor asked.

Sean nodded. "Christmas break? Yeah, I'm free."

"Listen, in your dad's stuff, there's one more thing I think you should have," Trevor said. He took a paperback book from his jacket pocket and handed it to Sean. Sean flipped through it and saw more of his dad's notations in the margins.

"The Lost City of Atlantis?"

"Read it on the plane, then we'll talk," Trevor said.

They all laughed. But Sean seemed distracted. Trevor looked down and saw that something inside Sean's bag was . . . moving!

"What are you doing?" Trevor asked.

"Uh, nothing," Sean said, quickly trying to close his bag. "Just feeding my . . . pet."

"What pet?" Trevor asked. "You don't have a pet."

The glowbird peeked its head out of Sean's bag and chirped.

Trevor couldn't believe it. "Sean!"

"Think my mom will let me keep it?" Sean asked.